THE GIRLS KNOCKED ON THE door. Rosemary Rita's heart was racing. Her mind was swirling. "Think fast. What am I going to say to Mimi?" Just in time a story came to her.

The door opened and a ten-year-old version of her grandmother was standing there. Her hair was longer and darker than now. Her cheeks were pink and she had freckles on her nose. She had the same warm blue eyes, but no glasses yet. Her skin was so smooth. She was so young. Rosemary Rita couldn't say a word. She just stared at her grandmother. This was by far the most amazing adventure yet—she and Mimi were so close.

"Mimi! Ooh—I can't believe I'm here," thought Rosemary Rita. She tried to control her breathing. She didn't want to sound like a puppy dog panting, but she was so excited it was hard to breathe normally.

The Hourglass

ADVENTURES SERIES

By **Barbara Robertson**

When my grandmother gave me an hourglass for my **tenth birthday**, I had no idea how amazing it really was. With it, I can travel back in time and **visit my ancestors**! Each generation of my family has one girl named Rosemary, and each one saved her postcards and trinkets from the special moments of her life. Now, those postcards are my **passport to adventure**! You can come along for the ride with the *Hourglass Adventures* books.

The adventure doesn't have to end when you finish the story! Visit my room at **winslowpress.com**, and you can check out fun facts, master games, send **cool coded messages** and cards to your friends, or just surf around and see what's new. You'll find quizzes, **craft ideas** and recipes, new mysteries, and great links all over the Web—your imagination is the only limit!

Read about the *Hourglass...*

In the *Hourglass Adventures* books, Rosemary Rita travels to amazing places and times. Online, you get to do the traveling with games, activities, interactive mysteries, and more. Throughout this story you'll find online activity prompts at the tops of the pages.

Costume Shop:
Dress up Rosemary Rita at winsl...

another
then

come up here. People are having too much fun for her taste. Besides, she doesn't think the cabins in second and third class are as comfortable. The Upper Deck is quite posh, you know."

"Oh, I think Gracie would like it here. She's so adventurous—"

"Gracie! You know my mother? And you call her Gracie?" May-May's eyebrows rose in disbelief.

"No, of course I don't know her. It's just that, um, James, well, he always refers to his Aunt Gracie as so much fun and everything. I guess I just *feel* that I know her." Rosemary Rita stumbled over her words as she tried to cover her mistake.

"It's true, James does get along well with

ano...
them
owne...
Precious...
"Hello...
friend and...
seems to like yo...
my girl has a boyfrien... ...must
get them together to play."

"Mrs. Harrington, I'm surprised to see you up here. I thought you would stay on the Upper Deck," said Rosemary Rita.

"Well, dear, I wanted my Precious to get a little direct sunlight, although I must say it is windy here. Then again, I'm a sturdy sort. As I always say, a little fresh air never hurt anyone." Mrs. Harrington chuckled as she spoke.

Precious and Snowball nuzzled up close to each other. Rosemary Rita introduced May-May to Mrs. Harrington. Then they all sat down on deck chairs. Mrs. Harrington pulled a red ball out of her coat pocket and tossed it to Precious. The dogs nudged the ball back and forth to each other.

36 · THE HOURGLASS ADVENTURES

ROSEMARY AT SEA · 37

Like what you see? Log onto **winslowpress.com** and you'll find Rosemary Rita's room, and all of the activities from this book. Click on the prompt from the page you're reading to play the game, solve the mystery, master the activity, and explore Rosemary Rita's world!

Click into your own adventure!

Visit the *Hourglass Adventures* Web site at winslowpress.com.
Click on the cover of the book that you want to explore.

Choose an activity from your book.

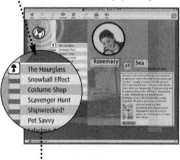

Check out all the web activities in this book:

ROSEMARY·AND·THE
ISLAND·TREASURE

BY BARBARA ROBERTSON

Hourglass Adventures

Nº 4

ROSEMARY
AND THE
ISLAND
TREASURE

WINSLOW PRESS

NEW YORK

Library of Congress Cataloging-in-Publication Data
Robertson, Barbara (Barbara K.)
Rosemary and the island treasure / by Barbara Robertson.—1st ed.
p. cm. – (The hourglass adventures ; #4)
Summary: Magically transported back in time to 1947, ten-year-old
Rosemary Rita searches for buried treasure with her grandmother,
also age ten, on the island Green Turtle Cay.
ISBN 1-890817-58-9
[1. Time travel—Fiction. 2. Magic—Fiction.
3. Buried treasure—Fiction. 4. Grandmothers—Fiction.
5. Green Turtle Cay (Bahamas : Island)—Fiction.] I. Title.

PZ7.R54466 Re 2001
[Fic] 21
2001045490

Creative Director
Bretton Clark

Book Designer
Annemarie Cofer

Web Site Designers
Annemarie Cofer
Patricia Espinosa

Web Programmer
John Fontana

Web Content Editor
Deirdre Langeland

PRINTED IN THE U.S.A
First edition, October 2001
2 4 6 8 10 9 7 5 3

WINSLOW PRESS
115 East 23rd Street, 10th Floor
New York, NY 10010

Discover *The Hourglass Adventures'* interactive Web site with
worldwide links, games, activities, and more at winslowpress.com.

To my darling husband,

Marsh—

my rock, my treasure.

Greetings From...
GREEN TURTLE CAY, 1947

"A Beautiful Place to Visit"

Chapter 1

LOOKING·FOR·MIMI

OSEMARY RITA HUNG UP THE phone and yelled downstairs for her mother. "Mom, where's Mimi? I've been calling her, and I keep getting her answering machine."

"I can't hear you! If you want to talk to me, come down here," her mother yelled back.

Rosemary Rita groaned. She grabbed her green velvet bag and ran downstairs to the kitchen to find her mother. "Mom, where's Mimi?" she asked again.

Rosemary Leigh Hampton put the last dish into the dishwasher, wiped her hands on a towel, and then turned to her daughter. "Don't you remember? Your grandmother left today for a business trip. She'll be in California for a couple of days."

"Can I call her there?"

"Sure, but she won't be there until 5:30 PM our time."

"Oh, no! I really want to talk to her." Rosemary Rita frowned. This was no time for her grandmother to be away.

"Is there something that I can help you with?" asked her mom.

Rosemary Rita shook her head and smiled to herself. This was definitely something she did *not* want to discuss with her mother! "Nah, it's all right. Thanks anyway. Guess I'll just go to The Rock," she said, heading out the back door.

Behind Rosemary Rita's home in Greenville, South Carolina, an enormous rock surface stretched out about fifty feet wide and forty feet long. Several large rocks were scattered on top of the area, creating a place to sit or climb. A forest of pine and oak trees began where the rock ended. It was a meeting place for the kids in the neighborhood. Known

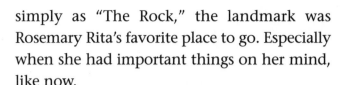
simply as "The Rock," the landmark was Rosemary Rita's favorite place to go. Especially when she had important things on her mind, like now.

Today was the fourth day of her spring break from school. With all of her close friends away, Rosemary Rita wasn't expecting to see anyone. She sat down on one of the large rocks and pulled a notepad and pen out of her bag. "I wish Mimi was home. She's the only one I can talk to about the hourglass," thought Rosemary Rita as she doodled a picture of it on her pad.

On her tenth birthday, just four days ago, Mimi had sent her ten boxes that had changed her life. Nine of the birthday boxes contained postcards, letters, newspaper articles, clothing, trinkets, souvenirs, and other special items that her ancestors, all named Rosemary, had saved over the years. Rosemary Rita was the sixth Rosemary in the family. She and her grandmother Mimi (Rosemary Regina) had always shared a special relationship. Now they shared a special secret: the secret of the magic hourglass!

In the very last box, wrapped in shiny red

paper, had been an antique hourglass. A picture of a man standing near a boat on the water was etched into the bottom of its stand. On the top of the hourglass were ancient letters and symbols. When Rosemary Rita held a postcard in one hand and flipped the hourglass over, she was transported back to the time and place of the postcard! She had already taken three adventures back in time, and she was anxious to go on another.

She made a chart on her pad. It read:

TIME and PLACE	Rosemary	AGE
1870 Berlin, Germany	Rosemary Ruth Berger	age 10
1889 Paris, France	Rosemary Grace "Gracie" Christianson	age 10
1919 The Mauretania	Rosemary Anna "MayMay" Gibson	age 10
1947 ???	Rosemary Regina "Mimi" Ryan	age 10

Rosemary Rita had already figured out that she was meeting each grandmother at ten years old. Next on the list would be Mimi! In fact, yesterday she picked through Mimi's postcards and found the perfect one.

She reached into her bag, pulled out the postcard, and read it one more time. The photograph on the front was of a colorful beach scene. It had the whitest sand and the bluest water she'd ever seen. On the back of the card was a message from Rosemary Rita's great-grandfather, Professor Frederick Ryan, to his daughter, Mimi.

October 16, 1947
To my dearest Rosemary,
Hello from the beautiful island of Green Turtle Cay! I have only been away a week, but I already miss you and your mother and brothers. I am counting the days until all of you join me in this paradise. I know that it is difficult to leave your friends and familiar surroundings. Keep in mind it will only be for a year. Also, this island is full of history and adventure. In fact, I found a treasure map at an outdoor market in town. I'm hoping the prospect of buried treasure will give you some-thing to look forward to and make leaving

easier. I am sending the treasure map so that you can study it closely and be prepared to search for the lost treasure when you arrive!
With love,
Daddy

Rosemary Rita smiled as she thought of her grandmother Mimi studying this same map all those years ago.

"I wonder if there really was a treasure and if Mimi ever found it," thought Rosemary Rita as she rummaged through her bag. She pulled out a yellowed piece of paper covered with numbers and drawings. It certainly looked like a real treasure map! Her heart beat faster as she stared at the drawings on the map. "I wish that I could talk to Mimi now. I can't wait four whole hours. Hey, wait a second. Maybe I *can* talk to Mimi right now. Or at least ten-year-old Mimi," she thought.

Rosemary Rita scooped up her notepad and pen, the postcards and map, shoved them into her bag, and raced back to her house. She ran through the kitchen door, buzzed by her two-year-old brother Ryan and her mom, and went straight to the den.

After searching the shelves, she grabbed an old family photo album, then raced up the stairs.

"Rosemary Rita," called her mother. "Where are you off to in such a hurry?"

"Nowhere, I'm just working on . . . a project in my room. I'll be down in about an hour or so," replied Rosemary Rita from the top of the stairs.

She headed down the hall to her room. Placing the bag on her four-poster bed, she started thumbing through the photo album. It had pictures of Mimi from when she was a little girl. Spidery script next to each photograph gave the details of the picture: "Rosemary and Daddy at the circus," "Rosemary's fifth birthday party," "Mimi and Eileen dressed for church." At last, she found the section she was looking for. Beside the pictures it said: "Mimi and new friends, Green Turtle Cay, 1947" and "Our house in Green Turtle Cay." Rosemary Rita gently plied the two pictures from their corner holders. In the first picture, Mimi was wearing a red, white, and blue dress and dancing around a pole with some other girls. The second photograph was of a white house with a red roof and bright green shutters.

Rosemary Rita stared intently at the photos. Then she jumped up and began shuffling through the birthday boxes, which were lined up against the wall. Each box was numbered. Box number four had the most clothing in it. Rosemary Rita rummaged through the box, sending clothing flying everywhere. Earlier, she had seen a red, white, and blue cotton dress that reminded her of the dress Mimi was wearing in the photograph. She had to find it!

When the pile of clothes out of the box was greater than what was left inside, she finally found it. Rosemary Rita let out a squeal. She quickly changed into it. Running her hands up and

down the dress, she tried to smooth out the wrinkles, but it was no use. Luckily, the dress fit her perfectly, even if she did feel like a cheerleader.

"I can't believe Mimi wore this!" She laughed as she looked at herself in the mirror. "I look like I'm wearing a flag!"

The dress had a V-shaped neck, and a tight waist, then flared out from the hips. There were wide red, white, and blue strips decorating the skirt.

Rosemary Rita played with her straight light brown hair. "How should I wear it?" she wondered. "Maybe I'll make pigtail braids. I could tie white ribbons to the end. I'm glad my friends aren't around to see me. Now, let's see, what else? Shoes. Can't wear my clogs. I guess I could wear my patent leather church shoes."

After she put on the shoes and fixed her hair, she looked in the mirror again. "That ought to do it," she said, and then walked back to her bed. Pulling open the drawstrings on her green velvet bag, she checked her supplies. Inside the bag she had about half a bag of Skittles, some warm Gatorade, cracker crumbs, and a small tape recorder. She dumped the crumbs and the Gatorade into the trash. Racing downstairs, she slowed as she neared the kitchen and peeked in to see if Mom and Ryan were still there. Luckily, they were not. She grabbed a bottle of Gatorade and a pack of peanut butter crackers, then darted back upstairs to her room. As she turned the corner she nearly plowed Ryan down.

"Hey, watch it, Row-may-we Wheat-a!" said Ryan.

"Sorry, buddy. I didn't see you. What are you doing?"

"I get my ball," he replied as he held his football up.

Their mom called from downstairs, "Ryan are you coming?"

"You'd better get going, Ryan. I'll see you later," Rosemary Rita said, giving her little brother a gentle nudge.

Ryan tugged at her dress. "You look funny."

"I know, I know. Now go see Mom," she said as she guided Ryan toward the stairs and headed to the safety of her room. "Phew! Good thing Mom didn't see me in this outfit. All right, I'm all set. Green Turtle Cay—here I come!"

Sitting on her bed, she pulled the map out of the bag. "Guess I'd better leave it here." She placed the bag on her lap. Then she picked up the postcard and the hourglass. Taking a deep breath, she turned over the hourglass.

As the sand in the glass started to drip down to the bottom, she felt funny, kind of light in the head. Her stomach felt queasy as if she'd just stepped off a roller-coaster ride. Suddenly, everything became blurry. She fell back onto the pillows. Before she knew it, she had fallen into a deep, deep sleep.

Chapter 2

BACK·IN·TIME

Slowly, Rosemary Rita opened her eyes. She was still a little woozy as she looked around. She was standing in the middle of a narrow road with rows of small houses on either side. The houses were painted white with brightly colored trim in pinks, greens, and blues. In front of each house was a neat fence. In the distance, she could see turquoise blue water. The sun was out, but it was breezy. Rosemary Rita pushed at her dress to keep it from blowing up.

The houses reminded her of her own doll house. It was like a town of doll houses all lined up in a row. No neon signs or Putt-Putt golf courses like at some of the beaches she'd been to. She didn't see any cars, trucks, or tourist buses. A few birds chirping broke the silence. There weren't any loud boom boxes or honking horns to disturb the peace.

Rosemary Rita thought of the long line of cars that they waited in each summer to get to the beach. This was much nicer.

Looking at the houses again, she felt a sudden twinge in her stomach. "Oh, no, *all* of these houses look like the one in the picture. How will I ever recognize Mimi's house? And what on earth am I going to say when I get there? Oh, brother, why don't I ever think of details?"

Just then a girl about her age came walking up the road. She had dark brown skin and black hair. She was wearing a flowered dress with a white apron and sandals. In her arms were bundles of bread.

"Excuse me," said Rosemary Rita. "Do you know where Professor Frederick Ryan lives?"

The girl paused and shifted the weight of her packages. Rosemary Rita wondered if she could understand her. During her other adventures, she had magically been able to speak the language of the place she landed. The girl looked like a native Bahamian. Rosemary Rita's thoughts were interrupted by the crisp British accent of the girl. "Yes, I know where Mr. Ryan lives. He's on my list of deliveries. My parents own the bakery in town. I help bring the bread 'round. I usually save the Ryans' for last so that his daughter and I can play while I'm there."

"His daughter? You know his daughter?" Rosemary Rita couldn't keep the excitement from her voice.

"Yes, she's my age. We met a few weeks ago when she arrived and have become quite good friends. If you'd like to come with me, you can. I only have two stops to make before the Ryans'."

"Oh, thank you. I'd love to."

"My name is Viola Cornish."

"Oh, what a beautiful name. My name is R-Ros-e—," she paused, trying to figure out what name she would use during this adventure.

"Hi, Rosie. Nice to meet you."

"Rosie? Rosie. Yep, that's my name. Nice to meet you, too." The girls walked up the steep unpaved road. Still no cars or trucks in sight. A few people walking or riding on bicycles passed them.

The first house they came to belonged to a man named Albert Lowe. Mr. Lowe was home and insisted on showing the girls his collection of large model ships. They were incredible, but Rosemary Rita was anxious to see Mimi. Soon Viola ended the chat, delivered her bread, and they were on to the next delivery. As they walked, Viola pointed to a big, two-story frame house. A beautiful garden was neatly defined inside the front fence.

"The Chamberlains used to live here. You know, Neville

Chamberlain, who was prime minister of England? He lived here as a boy. His family farmed pineapples on the island until they sold their business to the Doles of Hawaii. Now it's the New Plymouth Inn," Viola explained. "Is that where you're staying?"

"Um, yes," Rosemary Rita replied tentatively.

Viola darted ahead as they neared the next house on her list. Rosemary Rita quickened her pace to keep up. They walked to the door and Viola knocked. A heavy-set woman answered and Viola handed her the bread.

The third and final stop was the Ryans' home. Rosemary Rita sucked in her breath when she spotted the white clapboard house with the red roof and bright green shutters.

"That's the house!" she exclaimed.

"Yes, it is. I thought you didn't know which one it was," Viola commented.

"No, I, uh, meant, this must be the house," Rosemary Rita said. Viola gave her an odd look.

The girls knocked on the door. Rosemary Rita's heart was racing. Her mind was swirling.

"Think fast. What am I am going to say to Mimi?" she thought to herself. Just in time a story came to her.

The door opened and a ten-year-old version of her grandmother was standing there. Her hair was long and dark. Her cheeks were pink and she had freckles on her nose. She had the same warm blue eyes, but no glasses yet. Her skin was so smooth. She was so young. Rosemary Rita couldn't say a word. She just stared at her grandmother. This was by far the most amazing adventure yet. She and Mimi were so close.

"Mimi! Ooh, I can't believe I'm here," thought Rosemary Rita. She tried to control her breathing. She didn't want to sound like a puppy dog panting, but she was so excited it was hard to breathe normally.

Mimi didn't recognize her. Of course she wouldn't, but somehow Rosemary Rita hoped that she would.

Viola introduced her. Mimi held out her hand.

"I'm so glad to meet you, Mimi," said Rosemary Rita as she reached out to take

Mimi's hand. There were no wrinkles or brown spots on Mimi's hand. But it was warm and soft, just like always.

"Nice to meet you too, Rosie," replied Mimi as she led them inside. The three girls walked into the house. The ceilings were low and the rooms were small. Everything was neat and tidy.

"I met Rosie in the road. She was trying to find your house," said Viola.

Mimi raised her eyebrows in an arch as she looked at Rosemary Rita. "You were trying to find me? We've only been here a few weeks. You're lucky you ran into my only friend on the island." Mimi and Viola laughed.

Once again, Rosemary Rita had to bend the truth. She promised herself that this was a practice she would only employ during adventures and only because it was a necessity. The truth was stranger than fiction.

"That *was* good luck," said Rosemary Rita. "I'm here for a few days visiting. My father is making some deliveries from South Carolina. We're staying at the New

Plymouth Inn. The innkeeper told me that there was a girl about my age staying nearby and that I should try to find you." Rosemary Rita held her breath and hoped that this was a believable story.

"Oh, you must mean Mrs. Roberts. I see her when I'm taking my walks. She always asks me about a thousand questions."

"She told me you missed your friends at home," Rosemary Rita said.

"Mrs. Roberts was right. I really do miss them. And I'm so glad that she sent you," Mimi said, pointing to Rosemary Rita.

Rosemary Rita smiled brightly. She was relieved that Mimi had believed her story and happy to see her grandmother. She tried to take in every detail of the young Mimi without being too obvious.

"How would you like a tour of the island? We could ride bikes down to the dock," suggested Mimi.

"One problem," said Viola. "Rosie and I don't have bicycles."

"Not a problem. You can borrow my brothers' bikes. They went out in the boat with my father and won't be back until dark."

"Great, then what are we waiting for? Let's go," said Viola, skipping toward the door.

Rosemary Rita followed. Her heart was beating like a drum. She wanted to scream she was so excited. This was the coolest adventure yet!

Chapter 3

GREEN·TURTLE·CAY·1947

MIMI, VIOLA, AND ROSEMARY Rita climbed on the bikes and rode down the narrow dirt road toward the water. Several boats and sailing dinghies were tied to the docks. They hopped off the bikes and laid them on the ground.

"Viola, doesn't your family own one of these dinghies?" asked Mimi.

"Yes, that one over there," said

Viola pointing to the white dinghy on the end.

"Do you think we could take it out? I'd love to show Rosie the other side of the island. It has the prettiest view in the world."

"I think that would be fine. My parents don't mind if I use it as long as I'm careful," said Viola.

"Wow, that would be so cool!" said Rosemary Rita. She loved boats, but she'd never been out on a boat or a dinghy with just other kids before. The dinghy was different than the inflatable ones she'd seen. This one was made of wood. The outside was painted white and the inside was natural wood, polished and shiny.

"It is a little breezy today, but I don't think you'll be chilly. The sun is out."

"Huh? Oh, I see what you mean. I'm sure it will be perfect." Rosemary Rita thought to herself, "I need to be more careful what I say. Of course they don't know the word 'cool.' Me and my big mouth."

The girls climbed down from the dock into the boat. It wobbled back and forth

adjusting to the weight of its passengers. They sat down. Rosemary Rita held tightly to the sides. Viola and Mimi used the oars to guide them away from the Green Turtle Cay dock toward the other side of the island.

"Rosie, it is only a few minutes by boat, but if we rode our bikes it would take half a day," said Viola.

"I can't wait to see this part of the island. Does anyone live there?" asked Rosemary Rita.

"A few people are scattered about, but no one lives in my favorite part. There are several acres with nothing but trees and beach. Sitting on top of the hill are the remains of an old pineapple plantation. The house is almost completely gone, but I found a tunnel that must have led from the house to the root cellar. I love to go exploring there."

"Oh, Viola, that sounds so exciting—a secret tunnel. Can you take us there?" asked Rosemary Rita.

"Of course," said Viola. "I love any chance to go exploring on White Sound."

As the girls paddled along, Rosemary

Rita reached her hand into the cool water, then licked her fingers. The water tasted salty just like at the ocean in South Carolina. It was so much bluer, though. The water was so clear she could see all the way down to the bottom. In the distance, the white powdery beach shimmered. They arrived at the dock at White Sound just as a sailing vessel was pulling out. Inside the boat were three large men wearing pin-striped suits with wide lapels. They also wore the kind of hats Rosemary Rita had seen in old photos of her grandfather.

"Hmm," said Viola rubbing her chin. "That's strange. I've never seen anyone use this dock, especially wearing business suits. They must be visitors. No one gets that dressed up here. Oh, well, come on girls. I can't wait to show you my favorite spot."

The girls tied the dinghy to the dock, and then climbed up the hillside to Viola's hideaway. They sat at the top of the hill and looked around. All around them were pine trees. Below them, at the foot of the hill, was a stretch of pure white sandy beach. From every angle you could see the turquoise blue water. When the sun went behind a cloud the water would change color to a darker blue. The shallow water wove in with the deeper water to form a pattern of different shades of blue.

"I see why you like this place so much. It's the most incredible view I've ever seen. You can see for miles all around. I feel like we can reach up and touch heaven," said Rosemary Rita.

"At my favorite spot, I feel like I can touch the sky, too," said Mimi. "It's on the top of our apartment building in New York. I love to go up there. Mrs. Hodges, the lady who owns the penthouse, lets me water her flower garden. The view up there is wonderful. I can see Central Park and the Museum of Natural History. But it sure is different from here." Mimi grew quiet for a moment, then said softly, "Hmm, I wonder who's watering Mrs. Hodges's flowers now." She seemed sad.

Rosemary Rita looked at Mimi. She had remembered hearing about Mrs. Hodges and the beautiful flower garden on the rooftop. In fact, Mimi had a little garden of her own now at her apartment on Park Avenue. When Rosemary Rita visited Mimi, they spent a lot of time in the garden on the balcony. Mimi had even cut some of the lavender plant for Rosemary Rita to put in her drawer to make it smell nice.

"I love lavender," blurted Rosemary Rita.

Mimi looked at her with her eyebrows arched. "How did you know that Mrs. Hodges had lavender planted in her garden?"

"I didn't. I, uh, just thought of flowers and, um, sweet-smelling things and it made me think of lavender," Rosemary Rita said, stumbling over her words.

"It does smell great, doesn't it? One day, I'm going to have a garden with lavender in it," said Mimi.

"I bet you will," said Rosemary Rita. "I

know you will," she thought to herself with a chuckle.

"What's so funny?" asked Viola.

"Oh, nothing," replied Rosemary Rita. "I was just thinking of my favorite place. It's called The Rock. It's this enormous flat rock that covers the ground. On top of it are large rocks that you can climb or sit on. It's right behind my house. Sometimes, I meet my friends there. Other times, I go by myself to get away from my little brother."

"We're lucky that we all have a special place that we can go to," said Mimi. Turning to Viola, she added, "I may need to borrow your special place while I'm here. I miss mine more than I thought I would."

"It would be my pleasure to share it with you," Viola said with a big smile.

"Speaking of special places, can we go to the secret tunnel now?" asked Rosemary Rita.

"Absolutely. Let's go," said Viola as she pulled herself up.

As they stood to go, Mimi noticed a dark cloud lurking above them. "Oh, no. It looks like it's going to storm," said Mimi.

Viola glanced up and frowned. "You're right. We'll have to visit the tunnel another time. We'd better get back before the storm comes in."

The girls hurried down the hill and got in the dinghy. This time, Rosemary Rita offered to help row the boat. She had rowed a boat once before when her family visited Lake Jocassee. But these wooden oars were more difficult to maneuver and the water was so choppy. Her arms grew tired, but she didn't mind a bit. There was nothing in the world that she'd rather have been doing than sailing a little dinghy with Mimi and Viola.

In no time they were back at the Green Turtle Cay dock. A larger boat had arrived. Sweaty, shirtless men lifted crates out of the big boat. The girls paused to watch.

Viola said, "Looks like Captain Archer and the shipment from Nassau is in. My parents will be glad. We were down to our last twenty-pound bag of flour."

"Well, then I'm sure glad they'll be getting more. I don't know what I'd do without your

mother's delicious conch fritters!" said Mimi.

"Conch fritters? What are they?" asked Rosemary Rita.

"You've never had one?" asked Viola. "It's a kind of fried seafood. There are loads of conch on the island and it's used for just about everything. You see that wall over there?" Viola asked while pointing to a low pinkish cement wall that circled the building opposite the dock. Mimi and Rosemary Rita nodded. "Well, it was made with crushed conch shells. There are lots of dishes made with conch, but the fritters are my favorite, too. My mother makes delicious ones. Why don't we go to the bakery and get some now? All this talk about them is making me hungry," said Viola.

"Me, too," said Mimi. "Let's go."

"Sounds good to me," chimed Rosemary Rita. The girls found their bikes where they had left them and climbed on. They quickly pedaled the short distance from the dock to Viola's bakery. Viola led them to the back entrance of the bakery. They parked their bikes and went inside.

Chapter 4

TROUBLE·AT·THE·TEA·PARTY

MOTHER, I'M HOME," CALLED Viola as they entered the back room. There was no answer. Viola pushed open the door leading to the front of the store and motioned for the girls to follow. "Mother? Are you there? Papa? Anyone here?"

Rosemary Rita pointed to the front door. "Look. The 'closed' sign is up."

"Hmm, that's strange. They never close this time of day. Oh, well, maybe we missed them on their way to meet Captain Archer at the dock. I really am hungry. How would you like it if I fixed us a little tea party?" asked Viola.

Rosemary Rita's eyes grew big and she smiled broadly. "That would be great!"

"Thank you, Viola, that would be swell," added Mimi.

Viola hummed as she moved through the bakery gathering things. The girls followed her to the back of the shop. She placed a colorful cotton tablecloth on a wooden table. Then she put the water on to boil. She pulled out three plates, three tea cups, and three saucers from the cabinet.

"Can we help?" offered Mimi.

"No, I'm fine," said Viola. She placed some scones on a bigger plate and laid it on the table. She put some jam, butter, and a spoon next to the plate. "Mother's not here to make the fritters, but I thought you might enjoy some of her scones."

Rosemary Rita started to ask what scones were, but decided that the girls might wonder why she had such a limited knowledge of food. She thought about the food in her bag. Her mouth was watering for some Skittles. She decided that she had to have some and had enough to share.

"I have some candy in my bag, if anyone would like some," Rosemary Rita said as she pulled out a red bag of Skittles from the velvet bag. She put a handful on each of the three plates.

"I've never heard of that kind of candy," said Mimi.

"Maybe they just sell them in South Carolina," said Rosemary Rita, wondering if she'd made another blunder.

"Well, they sure are delicious!" said Viola as she popped a couple more into her mouth.

"Yes, they are yummy," added Mimi.

"Glad you like them. Now I can't wait to try one of these scones," said Rosemary Rita. Just as she put the pastry to her mouth, there was a loud rapping at the front door.

Viola stood to answer it. "Can't they read the sign?" she mumbled as she passed through to the front section of the bakery.

Rosemary Rita stood up and peeked

through the doorway. Through the glass window she could see three men wearing pin-striped business suits and hats. They looked like the same men from the dock at White Sound.

"Guess all that sailing made them hungry, too," she thought.

Viola opened the door a crack. "Sorry, we're closed."

The men exchanged glances. The short one had bushy eyebrows and greasy strands of black hair peeking out from under his hat. "We'll come back later, then," he said. As the men turned to leave, there was a loud clap of thunder. The rain started to pour. It was coming down hard. The men were getting soaked.

As Viola was shutting the door, the larger man approached. "Please let us come in. We'll leave when the rain lets up."

Viola hesitated. She looked at the men. Rosemary Rita noticed that although the men were nicely dressed, something about them made Viola uncomfortable.

Rosemary Rita could see a woman sloshing down the road. "Mother!" called Viola. When the men saw her, they left abruptly.

Ruby Cornish was soaked from head to toe. She was dripping water every- where. "Oh, Viola, I'm so glad you're here. Who were those men?"

"I don't know. They wanted something from the bakery, and I tried to tell them that we were closed. Then they wanted to come inside to get out of the rain. I'm glad you came home when you did," said Viola as she squeezed her mother tightly, wetting her own dress.

"Oh, sweetie, we've got big troubles." Mrs. Cornish's voice was tight and worried.

"What is it?" asked Viola.

Rosemary Rita and Mimi moved closer. "Viola, is everything all right?" asked Mimi.

"I'm not sure," Viola replied to the girls. Turning to her mother she said, "You know Mimi Ryan, and this is our new friend, Rosie."

Mrs. Cornish looked distracted. She mumbled, "Nice to see you. Excuse me, please, but I really must speak with Viola."

"That's all right. We'll wait in the other room," said Rosemary Rita.

Mimi and Rosemary Rita sat at the table.

"What do you think is the matter?" asked Rosemary Rita, drumming her fingers on the table.

"I don't know, but I have never seen Mrs. Cornish look so serious. She's usually so cheerful," said Mimi.

"They seem like a nice family."

"Oh, they are. I'd have died of loneliness by now without Viola. I was a little shy with her at first. I'd never had a colored friend before. But it didn't take me long to realize that I could have just as much fun with Viola as with my friends from home," said Mimi.

Rosemary Rita was trying to figure out

what Mimi meant when Viola came back into the room. There were tear stains on her face, and her smile was gone.

"My father's been arrested!" she stated.

"Oh, no!" exclaimed Rosemary Rita.

"*Your* father? It must be a mistake. He's so kind and gentle. What happened?" asked Mimi.

"My mother isn't sure. None of it makes sense. All she could figure out was that it had something to do with some visitors to the island. They accused Papa of stealing a gold watch. Officer Rogers said that he had no choice but to keep him in jail until the trial, unless we paid the bail money."

"How much is that?" asked Rosemary Rita.

"I don't know exactly. I do know we don't have it," said Viola as she started to weep again.

Mimi patted her shoulder, and Rosemary Rita handed her one of the napkins to wipe her eyes.

Mimi whispered to Rosemary Rita, "We've got to do something! I think I have an idea."

She turned to Viola. "Viola, I think I have something that can help your family. Can you come with us for a while?"

Viola shook her head. "I'd better stay here and help clean up and make sure my mother's okay first. How about if I meet you at your house in a couple of hours? I'll bring your brother's bike back then."

"That would be fine. We'll see you then." Mimi and Rosemary Rita hugged Viola, then walked out the back door and headed up the hill on the bikes. The rain had stopped, but their tires sprayed water as they passed through the puddles. Their shoes were getting soaked as they rode, but neither seemed to notice. Both girls were thinking about Viola.

"This is terrible. Poor Viola. I can't believe her father is in jail," said Rosemary Rita. She couldn't imagine how she'd feel if it was her dad!

"It must be a mistake. I've met Mr. Cornish a couple of times. Like I said before, he's such a kind man. He would never steal anything," said Mimi.

The girls reached Mimi's house, parked the bikes, and went inside. Mimi called for her mother, but there was no answer. "Oh, I forgot. Mother said that she would be having tea with Mrs. Johnstone."

Rosemary Rita was relieved. She still hadn't figured out what she would say to May-May, Mimi's mother, when she met her. "I wonder if May-May would even remember me?" thought Rosemary Rita. "It's been twenty-eight years for her since we sailed on the *Mauretania* together. Only yesterday for me, though!"

Mimi led Rosemary Rita up to her room. "Rosie, I'm going to show you something that is very important. You must promise not to tell anyone else about it."

"I promise," said Rosemary Rita as her heart leapt to her throat. "Please, be what I think it is," she thought.

Mimi reached under her mattress and pulled out a yellowed piece of paper.

Rosemary Rita held her breath. It was the treasure map!

Chapter 5

MIMI'S·MAP

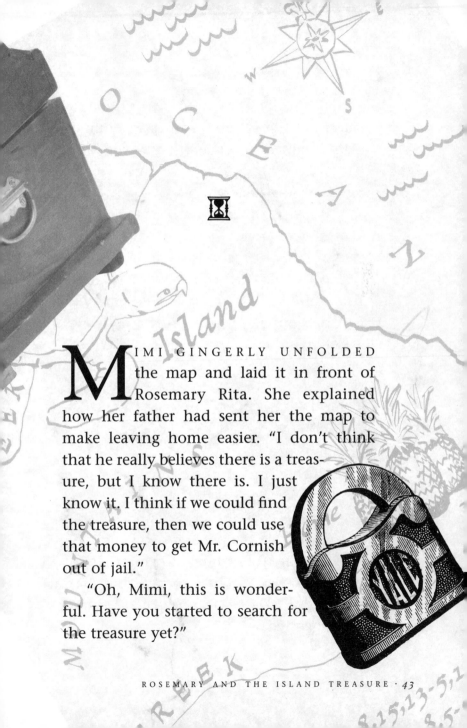

MIMI GINGERLY UNFOLDED the map and laid it in front of Rosemary Rita. She explained how her father had sent her the map to make leaving home easier. "I don't think that he really believes there is a treasure, but I know there is. I just know it. I think if we could find the treasure, then we could use that money to get Mr. Cornish out of jail."

"Oh, Mimi, this is wonderful. Have you started to search for the treasure yet?"

"Not really. It's kind of an unusual map. There are all of these pictures and numbers. I don't understand what they mean."

"We can figure it out, I know it. We're the best code crackers around."

"We are?" asked Mimi, raising her eyebrows in an arch.

"Ah, what I mean is we *have* to figure it out. It's Mr. Cornish's only hope. We need to have confidence," stammered Rosemary Rita. She had put her foot in her mouth again! Mimi and Rosemary Rita sent each other messages in secret codes back and forth from Greenville to New York. Of course, in Green Turtle Cay in 1947, Mimi was miles away from New York and years away from being a grandmother.

"I'll get some supplies so we can start trying to make sense of this map."

Mimi reached in her desk and pulled out several sheets of paper and two pencils.

Rosemary Rita studied the map carefully. It made no more sense to her now than it did earlier. "Let's take one part at a time," she suggested.

O C E A Z

N
W   E
S

CREEK

Island

MOUNTAINS

Home

CREEK

X

Potatoes and other vegetables are here

60-16,1,3,5,19-6,18,15,13-5,24,20,18,1,24,3,5-25,24
12,5,6,20-23,1,22,12-10,8,5-9,19-1-9,9,4,4,5,14-4,15
15,18,18,5,13,15,22,5-4,9,18,20-7,15-20,8,18,15,21,7
8-4,15,15,18,2,15,24-9,19-10-16,1,3,5,19-21,29,5-11,5
25-20,15-25,16,5,14,2,25,24

V.C.

V.C.

"I already figured out that the green turtle stands for Green Turtle Cay Island," said Mimi. "That was obvious, and it means that the treasure is buried on this island!"

"Great, now what about the potatoes and the pineapple?" asked Rosemary Rita. "Do you think the treasure is buried on a farm?"

"I don't know. I don't think farms were around in the 1700s when the pirates were here."

"Maybe the map wasn't made by pirates."

"You're right, just because it's a treasure map doesn't mean that pirates made it. Besides, there isn't a skull and crossbones anywhere on the map," said Mimi with a laugh.

Rosemary Rita laughed, too. "All right, let's skip the pineapple and potatoes for now. Look at all these numbers. We need to figure out what they mean."

"At first I thought they stood for how many paces we should walk, but there are too many numbers for that."

Rosemary Rita stared hard at the map,

Code Cracker:
Can you figure out the code at winslowpress.com?

her eyebrows furrowed together. Then she squealed. "I've got it! It's so simple. I use this code all of the time."

"What, what, tell me!" exclaimed Mimi.

"You see, each number stands for a letter of the alphabet. One is A, two is B, and so forth. What threw me was the number sixty. There are only twenty-six letters in the alphabet. But when you talked about the number of paces, then it all made sense."

Rosemary Rita scribbled on the paper, then showed Mimi her work.

"The first two words are: 'Sixty paces.' See, sixty is sixty, of course. Sixteen is P, one is A, three is C, five is E, and nineteen is S—paces. The commas separate the letters, and the dashes separate the words. Whoever wrote this made it easy. They wanted someone to figure out the message."

Rosemary Rita and Mimi set to work deciphering the rest of the letters. When they were finished, this is what they had spelled out:

> *Sixty paces from entrance on left wall there is a hidden door.*
> *Remove dirt, go through door. Box is ten paces.*
> *Use key to open box.*

"I still can't figure out what entrance they mean," said Rosemary Rita.

They were interrupted by a knock at the door. It was Viola. She looked sad and worried. She was twisting the hem of her dress with her fingers.

"Viola, you're just in time. How's your mother?" asked Rosemary Rita.

"She's still very upset. I don't know what to do."

"We might be able to help. I want to show you something," said Mimi, leading Viola to her room. "This is a treasure map that my father sent to me. I think if we could find the treasure, then we'd have enough money to get your father out of jail."

"Oh, Mimi, it is very sweet of you to want to help, but there are hundreds of fake treasure maps on the island. In the 1500s, Spanish galleons carrying treasure crashed on the coast of these islands. People have searched for hundreds of years to recover the treasure; a few have even been successful, but not many. I doubt that this is a real treasure map."

"Please take a look at it, Viola," urged Rosemary Rita. "Mimi and I have already decoded most of the map. Here's what we figured out." Rosemary Rita shared what the message said with Viola. She explained how they had figured out that each number stood for a letter.

"We're stumped by the pictures at the top," Mimi said, pointing to the pineapple and potatoes. "Do you have any idea what they mean?"

Viola looked at the pictures. "Pineapples are very common on the island. Remember I took you to the pineapple plantation on White Sound that had been torn down?"

"Of course! I wish we'd been able to go into the secret tunnel leading to the root place," said Rosemary Rita.

"Not root place, it's called a root cellar. It's where they kept their vegetables, like potatoes and onions."

"Viola, you are a genius!" said Rosemary Rita.

"I am? Why?" Viola looked from Rosemary Rita to Mimi.

"Look at the map. It has a picture of potatoes on it. Maybe the map is referring to your secret tunnel!" exclaimed Rosemary Rita.

"Oh, Rosie, you don't think it would be that easy, do you?" asked Mimi.

"It could be. It's not a very big island. How many pineapple plantations were there, Viola?" Rosemary Rita asked.

Viola was staring at the map. A strange look came across her face.

"Viola, Viola, did you hear me?" Rosemary Rita said.

"What? I was just looking at the key and these initials. I have a key just like this. It's been in my family for ages. My grandmother let me have it because it has my initials on it. See, here it is. I wear it for a good luck charm." Viola pulled at the ribbon around her neck and up came the key.

The girls gasped. "Oh, my goodness!" said Mimi. "The initials and the key are identical to the ones on the map. This is getting strange."

"I think it's getting exciting. Viola is somehow connected to this map. Maybe the treasure *is* buried in her secret tunnel. Can we go there now and check it out?" pleaded Rosemary Rita.

"Yes, let's go," said Viola. The girls ran down the stairs and out the door. They jumped onto the bikes and rode to the dock. Viola untied the dinghy and they got in. They took turns rowing, and in what seemed like no time they reached White Sound.

Chapter 6
THE·CHASE

THE GIRLS DOCKED THE DINGHY and ran up the hill to the former pineapple plantation. They stepped over what remained of the wall of the old house. Viola led them to the entrance of the root cellar.

"Watch your step," Viola called to the other girls as they headed into the tunnel.

Standing at the entrance, Rosemary Rita said, "Let's count out sixty paces."

They walked slowly, counting to sixty. It seemed to take forever, but finally they made it. All three of them got to work on the dirt wall on the left side of the tunnel. They scraped and scratched at it, but found nothing.

"Nothing's there." Viola sighed. "I knew it was too good to be true."

"Wait," cried Rosemary Rita. "Don't give up yet. It has to be here." She dug harder at the dirt.

"I'll help you, Rosie," said Mimi, using her shoe to bang the dirt off the wall.

Their fingers were dirty and getting sore. Viola started to cry again. "It's no use. There's no treasure down here. I'll never be able to help my father."

"It has to be here. I just have this feeling," said Rosemary Rita. "Maybe we didn't count right."

"Of course we did. We put one foot in front of the other and marched off sixty paces," said Viola.

"There's got to be something that we are missing. We walked the sixty paces—" said Mimi.

"That's it!" interrupted Rosemary Rita. "*We* walked the sixty paces, with our ten-year-old girl feet. Don't you see? Whoever wrote this map was probably a man with

man's feet. His paces would be bigger than ours. Let's try a little further down."

The three girls spread out farther along the dirt wall and vigorously scratched and clawed at the dirt.

Just as they were about to stop again, Rosemary Rita felt wood. "A door!" she yelled. "I found a door!" All three girls started scraping at the dirt with renewed energy. In a few minutes, they unearthed the hidden door. Together they heaved against it and pushed the door open. Dirt fell in their hair. Cobwebs blocked their way. Rosemary Rita panted, "Ten paces. We need to count out ten man paces, and we'll find the box."

Slowly they stepped one, two, three, four, five, six, seven, eight, nine, ten big paces from the door. "I'm scared to look," said Viola. "Is it there?"

Rosemary Rita kneeled down and felt around the ground with her fingers. She shrieked when she felt the metal box. "It's here! I found it."

"Can you lift it?"

"Yes, I think so. It's not very big." Rosemary Rita lifted the box.

"We should probably bring it out of the tunnel so we can see what's inside," suggested Mimi.

"Good idea." Rosemary Rita carefully held the metal box. She rubbed her fingers along the smooth metal. She imagined all of the wonderful things that could be inside.

The girls went back through the door and raced the sixty steps back to the entrance. They climbed the stairs up to what had been the kitchen of the plantation house. Rosemary Rita laid the box on the ground.

"Viola, do you want to try the key?" she asked.

"I'm too nervous. You do it," she said, yanking the key off her neck and handing it to Rosemary Rita.

Rosemary Rita sucked in her breath and pushed the key into the lock. It opened. The girls let out a whoop and screamed, "Hooray!"

She pulled open the lid. There were several papers and a

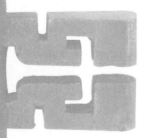

bag of gold coins, just like on the map.

"Wow! Look at these coins. I wonder what they are worth?" asked Mimi.

"I bet there's enough to get your father out of jail. Here, take them, Viola," said Rosemary Rita. Viola took the bag and shoved it in the pocket of her apron. "Somehow, they belong to your family. You had the key!"

"Maybe the papers will explain what they mean," said Mimi as she reached for the papers. "This one has the word 'deed' on top. I wonder why it's been cut in half like this?" Mimi held it up. It had been cut in a jagged pattern so that half of it was missing. "And there's a letter."

Rosemary Rita put the metal box down on the ground and looked at the map in her hands. She hated to admit it, but she was a little disappointed. She had imagined a much bigger treasure. "This wasn't exactly what I was expecting, but it's still pretty neat. I wonder what the deed is to?"

Just then the three men

that they had seen earlier came bursting out of the woods. Rosemary Rita quickly shoved the map into her green velvet bag. Mimi quietly slipped the deed and letter into her pocket.

"Miss, I believe you have something that belongs to me." The men glared at Rosemary Rita.

"No, I don't."

"Yes, you do. Now just hand it over and everything will be fine."

"You must be mistaken. I have nothing of yours," Rosemary Rita said, squaring her shoulders and standing up straight.

Just then the man with the bushy eyebrows lunged for her bag. She couldn't let him get it. If she lost the hourglass, she'd be stuck in the past forever.

Rosemary Rita screamed, "Run!" The girls took off. They scrambled over the remaining wall of the kitchen. They tried to avoid tree stumps and fallen branches. They circled back behind a pine tree.

Panting and out of breath, Rosemary Rita said, "Is everyone all right?"

"I'm scared," said Viola, her lips quivering.

"Me, too," chimed Mimi. "How did they find out about the treasure?"

"Beats me. We can't let them get it. Viola, is there another way out of here?" They could hear the branches and leaves crackling around them. The men were approaching. They needed to hurry. "Quick, help me grab this log." The girls hoisted the log and moved it directly in the men's path. Then they took off for their dinghy.

They could hear the men shout and curse as they stumbled over the log. Finally, the girls reached the boat. Viola struggled to untie the knot, but it wouldn't budge.

"Come on, Viola. Hurry!" yelled Mimi.

"I'm trying, it's stuck," panted Viola as she struggled with the rope.

The men were closing in on them. Just as they neared the boat, Viola undid the rope. The girls jumped in the dinghy and started to row. But one of the men dove in the water and swam to them. He lunged forward and grabbed Rosemary Rita's green velvet bag right out of her hands.

She screamed, "Stop! Please!"

The men quickly waded through the

water. The other two were ready to go. He climbed into the bigger boat and they were off. The girls tried to calm Rosemary Rita.

"I'm sorry they got your bag, but at least they didn't get the gold coins or the papers. We don't need the map anymore, we've already found the treasure."

Rosemary Rita was shaking. She tried to steady herself. She took a deep breath and then slowly blew it out. She started tapping her foot on the floor of the boat in a nervous patter. "My bag, my bag, I've got to get my bag back. We need to follow them."

"Follow those three huge men? Are you serious? Those candies you have were good, but not worth risking our lives," said Mimi.

"They wouldn't see us. If we could find out where they are staying, maybe we could sneak in and get my bag back. I have other things in there besides the Skittles. I have a birthday present from my grandmother. It's very special to me."

"I'm not sure, Rosie. That sounds far too dangerous to me," said Viola.

"We'll be careful. I don't think they were planning to hurt us, they just wanted the treasure. I'm sure when they find the map, they'll toss my bag aside and we can pick it up and get out of there unnoticed."

"If we find them, that is."

"We'll find them. Someone has to know where they're staying. You said so yourself, Viola, that it was unusual for men to be wearing business suits on this island. They must be from somewhere else. Besides the New Plymouth Inn, where else do visitors stay on the island?"

"If they're not staying at the inn, then they would have to be staying in someone's house. That could be anywhere." Viola sounded ready to give up, but Rosemary Rita was insistent.

"Well then, first we need to check at the inn," said Rosemary Rita.

The girls quietly rowed back to the dock. As they stepped out of the boat, Rosemary Rita grabbed their arms. "Look over there at the end of the dock. Do you see what I see?"

"It's the boat that the men were on, and it's tied to that huge houseboat!" said Mimi.

"That must be where they're staying," added Viola.

"Exactly."

"Boy, this is some strange day. First we're chasing a treasure, then we are being chased by treasure hunters, now we're chasing the chasers. I sure hope they don't catch us," said Mimi.

"They won't catch us. But just in case, maybe we should hide the papers and the coins before we go in," suggested Rosemary Rita. "Mimi, do you have a safe place to hide things?"

"Just at my house. My mother might be there, though—"

"Then we can't go there," interrupted Rosemary Rita.

"Rosie, don't sound so frightened. She doesn't bite." Mimi laughed.

"I'm sorry. Guess I'm getting a little jumpy." Rosemary Rita thought to herself, "I can't run into May-May. Even though it's been twenty-eight years since she's seen me, I wouldn't want to take any chances that she'd recognize me."

Viola was wringing her skirt into a knot

around her fingers again. "Rosie, I've been thinking. I don't want to go on that boat. With my father in jail, I'm all that my mother has. I have to take care of myself. I'm sorry, but I just can't go."

Rosemary Rita wrapped her arm around Viola's shoulders. "That's all right. I understand. Maybe that makes more sense, anyway. If we don't come back right away, you can go get help. And you can keep an eye on the coins and the papers."

"Phew, I'm glad that's settled," sighed Viola, releasing her tight grip on her skirt.

"Mimi, how about you? Are you coming?" asked Rosemary Rita.

"I can't let you go in all by yourself. I'll come," Mimi said as she reached in her pocket to retrieve the deed and the other papers. "Here, Viola, you take these."

Rosemary Rita hugged her. "You're the greatest."

The girls gave Viola a quick hug good-bye and then sat down on some crates to figure out a plan.

"How are we going to get inside without them seeing us?" asked Mimi.

"Good question," replied Rosemary Rita, tapping her foot on the wooden crate. Then she jumped up. "I've got it!" she exclaimed.

"What?"

"We can use these crates. We can hold them up to cover our faces as we walk closer to the boat. Then we can sneak up and run through the door."

Mimi let out a laugh and covered her mouth with her hands. "Oh, two girls walking with crates in front of their faces, that won't draw any suspicion."

Rosemary Rita couldn't help it, she had to laugh at the ridiculousness of her plan. But she was desperate. She had to get on that houseboat and find her hourglass. "All right, I see your point. Can you think of an idea?"

The girls looked at the large white houseboat only a few yards away. It was docked between two long wooden ramps. Rosemary Rita guessed that it was about the size of two back-to-back school buses. It had a wide bottom and a second story rising up from the middle.

"No, Rosie, I really can't think of anything," said Mimi, biting on her fingers.

"Then the only thing for us to do is to tip-toe up to the boat and try to get onboard without them seeing us. Look at the upper deck of the boat. I think I can see them."

Mimi glanced up at the top of the boat. "I do see them. It looks like they're sitting at a table eating. I'm glad that all this hasn't affected their appetite."

Rosemary Rita let out a nervous laugh. "Judging from their size, it looks like they've never missed a meal. What do you think? Will you come with me?"

"All right, I guess. I'll give it a try. But one thing, what do we do if they spot us?" said Mimi.

"The only thing we can do. Scream for help and run as fast as you can. I'm sure we're quicker than they are!"

Rosemary Rita reached for Mimi's hand and gently pulled her toward the end of the deck. They moved as quietly as they could. As they neared the edge, Rosemary Rita tried to peep through the window on the door of the boat.

She could see a long hall, a ladder going to the upper deck, and some closed doors.

Carefully, she turned the handle of the door and pushed it open. She felt that now-familiar pounding of her heart in her throat. She tried to focus all of her energy on finding her bag and the hourglass.

"If we don't find it right away, maybe we could come back tomorrow and go in when they're gone," whispered Mimi as they headed into the hall of the boat.

"Okay, but I'm really hoping that we find the bag. I don't think I'll sleep a wink without it." Rosemary Rita swallowed hard, thinking about the possibility of being stuck back in time. Tiny beads of sweat gathered on her forehead. "Can't think about that now. It's NOT going to happen," she thought.

The girls walked quietly down the hall. Without making a sound they entered the kitchen. They could faintly hear the men's voices above them. They searched all around the kitchen. No bag. They looked around one of the bedrooms. No luck. They passed by the ladder that led upstairs through a hole in the ceiling. The men's voices were getting louder. They must be directly above them. Rosemary Rita's heart was pounding so hard, she thought it might burst through her skin like a rocket ship. They quietly opened the next door.

"Mimi, it's there!" Rosemary Rita whispered, pointing to the floor. The bag had been tossed on the floor. Rosemary Rita flew to the bag, picked it up, and checked inside. The hourglass was still there! She felt around in the bag. The map was there, too.

"I'm surprised they didn't take the map out of the bag," said Mimi.

They heard footsteps coming down the ladder. "Quick, into the closet," whispered Rosemary Rita.

The girls scrambled into the closet and held their breath.

"I don't see the bag. Are you sure you left it here?" one of the men asked.

"Maybe I left it in the kitchen. We can get it in the morning."

"Sylvester!" yelled a third man.

"Yeah. In here, Jonathon," replied Sylvester.

More plodding footsteps. The third man joined them. The girls were afraid to move.

They stood frozen in the closet and listened.

"Those silly girls. How could they confuse some phony map for a deed?"

"Who knows? We still need to find the other half of that deed before Cornish does. Once we destroy the deed, we can claim the land."

"How exactly are we going to do that?"

"Don't you ever listen? Once we have both halves of the real deed, we destroy it. Then we create a fake deed, almost identical to the real one, but with one minor difference. Instead of title to the land belonging to the heirs of Jeremiah Cornish, it would belong to the heirs of Jonathon Snipes."

"Why can't it be in my name?"

"You idiot, Ralph, it doesn't matter whose name the deed is in as long as we get the land. Then we can mow down the trees and start building our resort and casino. And in no time, we'll be filthy rich."

Rosemary Rita had an idea. Turning slightly away from Mimi, she reached in her bag and pressed the record button on her tape recorder.

"What about Cornish? Do you think he

knows that it was us who planted the gold watch on him?"

"Of course Cornish doesn't know that we framed him. As long as he's in jail for stealing, he'll also never know that he is the owner of eleven acres of very valuable oceanfront land. I plan to keep it that way, so let's stop all of this talk."

"You don't have to be so snappy, Jonathon."

"It's been a long day. I didn't plan on having to chase little girls down the hillside. Let's go to the pub and get a pint."

The men filed out the door and off the boat. The girls waited an extra ten minutes to make sure that they were really gone before they stepped out of the closet. They quickly ran off the boat and back to Viola's house.

Chapter 7

THE·POLICE·STATION

VIOLA HUGGED THE GIRLS WHEN they walked through the door. "I'm so glad to see you. I was worried sick," she said.

"We're fine. We got the bag just in time."

"And we overheard them talking about your father. We need to take those papers to the police station right away. Those men framed your father to keep him from getting those papers."

"They admitted to framing him?" asked Viola.

"Yep, they did, and we can prove

it," stated Rosemary Rita. They explained everything they had overheard. Viola grew more and more excited as she listened.

"It's our word against theirs. Do you think the police are going to believe us?" asked Mimi.

"I think they will," said Rosemary Rita, confidently patting the bulge of the tape recorder in her bag.

The girls walked up the street to the tiny police station. It had two desks on either side of the room. Behind each desk sat a man in a gray uniform. Viola led them to the taller, lankier man, who had gray hair and long side burns. He was leaning back in his chair chewing on a piece of straw.

"Excuse me, Officer Rogers," said Viola.

"Hello there, Viola. I'm sorry about your father, but I can't let you see him. Visiting hours are over."

"Officer Rogers, my father didn't steal anything. The men who accused him planted the watch on him."

"Why would they do that?" asked Officer Rogers.

"We have some very important papers

that you need to see right away. I think it might explain things."

"Oh, you do, eh?" he said with a grin on his face.

The girls pulled out the map, papers, and coins and laid them on the desk. Officer Rogers read the papers. The expression on his face changed as he read. He tapped his fingers on the desk.

"Where did you get these papers and these coins?"

"Well, my father gave me a map that he bought in town," said Mimi.

"We wanted to find the treasure for Mr. Cornish's bail," added Rosemary Rita.

"The most amazing thing is that Viola had the key to the box! It's been in her family for years. She's somehow connected to the box," said Mimi.

"It's not that amazing when you read this letter attached to the deed. It's from Victor Cornish," said Officer Rogers.

"Victor Cornish? Who's that? I don't remember being told about any relatives named Victor," said Viola.

"Well, he wasn't related to you exactly.

You see he owned the large pineapple plantation on White Sound. Your ancestors were his slaves."

"Slaves! You mean Viola's family took the last name of the man who owned them?" asked Rosemary Rita.

"How horrible," said Viola. "I guess that's why Papa never talks much about his family history."

"Viola, it was horrible that people were used as slaves, but Victor Cornish was not a horrible man. In fact, he loved your family very much; so much that he left all of his land and his treasure to your family. Here, read this letter."

Viola took the letter. Mimi and Rosemary Rita stood on either side of her. They read the words that Victor Cornish had written over one hundred and fifteen years ago.

"This is incredible," said Viola. "Why didn't we find out about this sooner?"

"It was tricky back then. Slaves couldn't own land in 1832. He created this map and apparently gave it to your ancestor, Jeremiah Cornish, along with the key. Somehow, the map was lost. It's obvious from the letter that it was his hope that when slaves were free and allowed to be land owners, that Jeremiah or his heirs would inherit the land."

"Oh, this is so exciting! The land that you love is truly yours," said Rosemary Rita.

"Yes, and those men can't turn it into a resort and casino," added Mimi.

Officer Rogers looked at them. "What men? What are you talking about?"

The girls explained about seeing the men at White Sound, the chase, and overhearing them on the boat. Rosemary Rita was ready to pull out her tape recorder, and play the recording of the men talking. Luckily, that wasn't necessary. Officer Rogers believed them.

"Koop, go get Cornish and bring him to me," said Officer Rogers to the other policeman.

Rosemary Rita squeezed Viola's hand. They had done it. They had helped get Mr. Cornish out of jail.

Viola's father walked into the room. He was a tall man with dark skin and short black hair. His smile grew big when he spotted his daughter. He raced over to her and scooped her up in his arms. Rosemary Rita and Mimi smiled as they looked on.

Officer Rogers explained the whole situation to Viola's father and apologized for the misunderstanding. He promised that they would find and arrest Jonathon Snipes and his gang immediately. The girls and Mr. Cornish started for the door.

"Wait!" called Officer Rogers.

"What is it?" asked Rosemary Rita.

"I thought that you might want to take these papers and this bag of coins."

"Oh, my goodness," said Viola, her hand flying to her mouth. "How could we forget these?"

Officer Rogers handed everything to Mr. Cornish. "You might want to get those coins checked out. If I'm not mistaken, they could be

Spanish coins from the eighteenth century."

"Pirate treasure!" screamed Rosemary Rita.

"Sh, young lady. I wouldn't say that too loudly if I were you, but, yes, that's exactly what it could be."

Officer Rogers waved to them as they left. Once they were outside everyone started talking at once.

"Oh, Papa, I'm so glad that you're okay," said Viola.

"Where did you ever find those papers and the coins?" said Mr. Cornish.

"Pirate treasure. I knew that there was a real treasure," Mimi breathed excitedly. Her eyes sparkled.

"I think there's more," said Rosemary Rita.

Everyone stopped talking and turned to Rosemary Rita. "Rosie, what did you say?" asked Viola.

"I said that maybe there's more treasure.

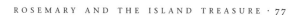

I keep thinking of Victor Cornish's letter, especially the last sentence. Maybe Victor Cornish found a chest of pirate treasure and the coins were only part of it. The rest could be hidden on his plantation," said Rosemary Rita.

"All those years ago. . . . Nobody has ever found it. How would we find it?" asked Viola.

"I want to take a closer look at the metal box that we found in the tunnel. Maybe there'll be a clue in the box that we missed before," said Rosemary Rita.

Mr. Cornish agreed to let the girls go if they promised to be careful. He wanted to see his wife and let her know that he was all right, then he would meet them at White Sound.

The girls sprinted to the dinghy and rowed toward White Sound. They were so focused on getting there, they didn't notice that another boat was following them!

Chapter 8
HIDDEN·SURPRISES

THE STORM HAD passed, but the wind had picked up again. The girls struggled to row the boat against the current. Rosemary Rita held her stomach as they bounced along the choppy water. Finally, they reached the dock at White Sound. Viola tied up the boat and the three girls walked back to the old pineapple plantation.

"First, we should read the letter from Victor Cornish again. Tell me what you think about that last sentence," said Rosemary Rita.

Viola pulled out the letter. "I still can't believe that this land belongs to my family.

I hope that my father rebuilds the house right on this very spot. Okay, here's the letter," said Viola as she handed it to Rosemary Rita.

March 2, 1832
Dear Jeremiah,
Every day that I wake up, I fear it will be my last. I do not have much time left. I want you to know how deeply I care about you and your family. Since my wife died, you are the only family that I have. Your father took care of us for many years. You have always been faithful to me. It has been almost six years since your father died and I gave you your freedom. I'm honored that you never left me, even though you were free to go.

You lived here and cared for this land all of your young life. There is no one else that I would rather have this land than you and your family. Unfortunately, people are ignorant and stubborn. It is against the law for you to own land at this time. I am hiding one half of the deed to this house and land in a box. I will give you a map to find it. I hope that this keeps the deed safe from those who may not want you to have the land. It is my sincere wish that you and your children and your children's children live in this beautiful place.

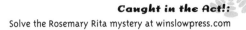

*Thank you for all that you and your family
have done for me.
Most sincerely,
Victor Cornish*

*P.S. One piece of important advice, it is never
wise to put all of your eggs in one basket.*

"The last line is strange, but I didn't see any hidden message in it," said Mimi.

"I've been thinking about the last line. I think that's our clue. Think about it, Victor warns Jeremiah not to put all of his eggs into one basket," said Rosemary Rita.

"Okay, I'm thinking about it, but I still don't see what that has to do with anything."

"All right, suppose we change the word "eggs" to "gold coins." Now do you see what I mean?"

"Oh, I do see. Victor Cornish is suggesting that he might have followed his own advice and not put all of the coins in the box."

"Yes, that's it, exactly! Now, we just need to figure out where the other basket is," said Rosemary Rita.

"I think we should start with the original box," suggested Viola.

"Great idea, Viola. It should be around here somewhere. I know we pulled it out of the tunnel."

The girls looked around. Rosemary Rita yelled, "There it is. I see it!" The girls ran to the box. There was a rustling in some bushes nearby.

"Did you hear that noise?" asked Viola. The girls stopped and listened but they heard nothing more.

"It was probably some little animal or something. Nothing to worry about," said Mimi.

"I suppose you're right," said Viola.

Rosemary Rita opened the box and felt along the sides with her fingers. "Nothing else here," she said as she passed it to Mimi.

There was a loud thump behind them. Mimi screamed and dropped the box. The girls looked around. "What's going on?" asked Mimi.

"I don't see anything. Don't worry," said Viola.

"Mimi, Viola, look! The box has a secret compartment. It fell open when you dropped the box," squealed Rosemary Rita as she pulled the piece of paper out of the compartment. She read it aloud.

"Ten more steps and the rest is yours."

The girls shrieked. "The rest of the treasure! We've found it," exclaimed Viola.

Just then, there was a loud noise and the three men burst out of the bushes. The girls screamed.

"Thank you, young ladies, for leading us to the treasure. We didn't even know about it. Now that you stole the deed from us, we'll settle for a chest of treasure." The man with the large nose snickered.

Rosemary Rita took a deep breath. Viola and Mimi were clinging to her. "What makes you think there is a treasure?" She was trying to stall for time.

"We've been listening. We started thinking about the map we saw in your bag and wondered if maybe it was real after all. We've come prepared," said the man, pointing to three large shovels.

"So, tell us what this ten steps means? Ten steps from where?"

"Ten steps from where we found the box is the rest of the treasure," said Rosemary Rita.

Mimi elbowed Rosemary Rita. "What are you doing?" she whispered.

"Don't worry. I've got a plan," Rosemary Rita whispered back.

"What are you two talking about?" asked Sylvester.

"Nothing. She didn't think that I should tell you where the treasure is," said Rosemary Rita.

"You're making the right decision. Just lead us to the treasure and nobody will get hurt," said Ralph.

"Well, we are very close to the spot. Come on, I'll show you," said Rosemary Rita as she led the men away from the root cellar door toward the other remaining wall of the house.

The men followed her closely. She noticed a hole where a tree had been uprooted. She stopped and pointed to the random spot.

"Here's where we found the box."

"Then we need to go ten steps from here," said Jonathon.

They walked ten steps. "Jonathon, I don't see anything," said Sylvester.

"You don't think that he would have left it out in the open, do you?" replied Jonathon, giving Sylvester a quick slap in the chest. "The treasure must be buried. We'll have to dig."

"Well, you don't need us anymore, so we'll be going," said Rosemary Rita as she started to walk away.

"Just a minute!" said Jonathon, pulling a pistol from his pocket and pointing it straight at the girls. Viola let out a gasp. Mimi and Rosemary Rita held each other tightly.

"How do we know if this is really where the treasure is buried? You three stay put until we find out."

Chapter 9

THE·TREASURE

THE GIRLS SLUMPED TO THE ground and clung to each other. Jonathon swung the pistol around their noses one more time, then shoved it back into his pants. The men picked up shovels and started digging for the treasure.

"What do we do now?" asked Viola.

"I'm not sure, but I'll think of something," said Rosemary Rita in a voice that sounded stronger than she felt.

The men shoveled and shoveled. The piles of dirt grew bigger. The men were getting sweaty and tired.

"I don't think there's anything here," said Sylvester, angrily.

Mimi whispered to Rosemary Rita and Viola. "I'm scared. What if they shoot us when they don't find the treasure?"

Rosemary Rita replied, "I think I've got a plan. I'm going to throw a rock at the wall over there. When it lands, it will make a loud noise. The men will turn to see what's there, and we'll make a run for it."

"I don't know, Rosie. What if we don't get away this time?" questioned Viola.

Rosemary Rita squeezed their hands. "I'm afraid this is our last chance. Come on, we can do it!" She lifted the rock and threw it as hard as she could at the wall. It made a crashing sound and the girls took off. They ran as hard as they could. All of a sudden they went slamming into several large men. They screamed.

Mr. Cornish said, "Don't worry, girls. It's just us."

Rosemary Rita spoke up. "Those are the men we were talking about. Quick, catch them. They're getting away!"

But Officer Rogers had come prepared. He had brought Deputy Koop and several men from town who were on the other side of the ruins, ready to apprehend the men. They captured them without a problem.

"Oh, Papa, I've never been so happy to see you," said Viola as she wrapped her arms around her father.

"I'm glad you girls are all right. Those are some dangerous characters. What were they digging for?"

"Oh, that was Rosie's idea. She told them that the treasure was buried there."

"That's what we told them, but I think I know where the treasure is *really* buried. Come on," said Rosemary Rita as she led the group back to the root cellar.

They opened the door, went down the steps, and walked the sixty paces to the secret door. Once inside they walked ten paces to where the box was first found. Then they walked ten more steps and bumped into a wooden box.

"Ah! There it is! We found the pirate treasure!" screamed the girls.

"Don't get too excited. Anything could be in there," said Mr. Cornish. They lugged the heavy box through the root cellar and up the stairs and outside.

Officer Rogers hit the lock with a shovel and Mr. Cornish opened the lid. Everyone gasped. The box was filled with glimmering gold coins, hundreds of them. They glistened in the sunlight, sending off a golden hue.

"Look at it. I've never seen anything so incredible," gushed Mimi.

"I can't believe there really was a treasure. I thought the land itself was enough, but this is too much!" exclaimed Viola.

"It really is amazing. I can't wait to tell my dad all about it. Speaking of him, I'd better get going. I bet he's looking for me," said Rosemary Rita.

"Do you have to go? I want to stay a little longer with the treasure," said Mimi.

"I can give her a ride back," offered Officer Rogers.

"Oh, thank you. That would be great." Rosemary Rita hugged Viola. Then she turned to Mimi. She took a last long look at her young grandmother with the dark hair and smooth skin. She gave her a big hug. "I'm glad that I'll be able to see you soon," she thought, "but I sure will miss having you to play with."

Rosemary Rita was quiet as Officer Rogers

rowed her back to the other side of the island. She replayed the events of the day in her head. What an adventure! She wondered what would become of the treasure. She was tempted to stay a little longer to find out, but knew she'd better not push her luck. When they reached the shore and docked the boat, Rosemary Rita thanked the kind sheriff and ran off behind a palm tree. She reached into her velvet bag and found the hourglass. Taking one long, last look around, she made a picture in her mind of beautiful, unspoiled Green Turtle Cay. Then she took a deep breath and flipped the hourglass over.

As the sand in the glass started to drip down to the bottom, she felt funny, kind of light in the head. Her stomach felt queasy as if she'd just stepped off a roller-coaster ride. Suddenly, everything became blurry. Before she knew it, she had fallen into a deep, deep sleep.

Chapter 10

HOME·AGAIN

WHEN ROSEMARY RITA WOKE up, she was relieved to find that she was back in her room. "I did it! I went back in time all by myself. Wait till I tell Mimi." Rosemary Rita glanced at her clock. It read: 2:58 PM. Once again, only an hour had passed. But still there were two and a half hours until she could talk to Mimi. Rosemary Rita slipped off the red, white, and blue dress and put her blue jeans and green sweater back on. Looking at her- self in the mirror, she noticed that her braids were a mess and she'd lost the ribbons. She undid the braids and brushed her shoulder-length brown hair.

Flopping down on her bed, she stared at the clock. Only seven minutes had passed. "Argh," she moaned. "I can't stand waiting."

She hopped up from the bed and went downstairs. Ryan was playing with blocks in the playroom. Her mom was working on the computer in the next room.

Rosemary Rita was dying to talk to someone about her adventure. She thought about confiding in her mother. "She'll never believe me. And if she does, she'll probably take the hourglass away."

"Is that you, Rosemary Rita?" called her mother.

"Yes, ma'am," she answered as she headed into the den.

"I just got an e-mail from Mimi. She took an earlier flight to San Francisco. She's there's now. You can call her on her cell phone, if you want," said her mother.

"She's there! I'll call her right now. Thanks, Mom." Rosemary Rita raced upstairs to use the phone in private. Her heart felt like it was pounding in her throat as she dialed Mimi's number.

"Hello," said the familiar voice at the other end of the phone.

"Mimi! It's you. I'm so glad to talk to you."

"Rosemary Rita. What's going on? You sound out of breath."

"I guess I am. Mimi, don't be mad at me, okay?"

"Sweetie, you know that I never get angry with you. Tell me what happened."

"Mimi, I took another adventure."

"You did? Where did you go? Who did you meet?"

"I met you, Mimi! You were so young and pretty. I mean, you're still pretty. But you were ten years old. We had a great time together."

"Oh, Rosemary Rita, that's so exciting. Did you go to New York?"

"No, I went to Green Turtle Cay."

"Oh, that's right. We moved there in late October of 1947, when I was ten. Isn't the island beautiful?"

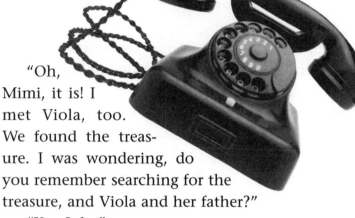

"Oh, Mimi, it is! I met Viola, too. We found the treasure. I was wondering, do you remember searching for the treasure, and Viola and her father?"

"Yes, I do."

"Mimi, do you remember meeting me?"

"You know, I think I do. It's so long ago, and of course back then I didn't know who you were. But I do remember another girl being there. She came to my house with Viola."

"It was me! This is too cool."

Rosemary Rita described every detail of her adventure. Mimi interrupted now and then with questions.

When she finished filling Mimi in on everything that had happened in Green Turtle Cay, Rosemary Rita had some questions. "Mimi, what happened to the treasure? Did the Cornishes get to keep it? How about the land? And Viola?"

"Slow down, honey. One question at a time. The land was legally the Cornishes. Under the law, they were allowed to keep the treasure as well. With some of the money, they rebuilt the plantation house and built a brand new schoolhouse. They also helped many families who still had not recovered from the terrible hurricane of 1932. My father helped them research the origin of the treasure and they donated some of the coins to a museum."

"Oh, Mimi, that's so wonderful. I knew that they were good people. What about Viola? Do you know what happened to her?"

"As I matter of fact, I do. We've kept in touch over the years. She married a very nice gentleman from Marsh Harbor and they have five children. She stayed in Green Turtle Cay and lived on the plantation with her parents, husband, and the children. She taught for many years in the schoolhouse that they built. She now has twelve grand-children."

"Wow. I'm glad that you're still friends

with her. That reminds me of something that you said in 1947. You called Viola and her family 'colored.' I think I've heard that term before, but I'm not sure what it means."

"When I was a young girl, many people referred to black people as 'colored' people."

"That's weird. It makes it sound as if they are drawn with crayons."

Mimi sighed. "Yes, but that's not the worst part. They were also treated differently. In some parts of our country African Americans were not allowed to vote, ride in the front of the bus, or go to school with white children. They didn't change the laws until around the time your mom was born."

"I've learned about some of that in school. It's incredible to think it wasn't even that long ago."

"I was lucky to know Viola when I did. It taught me that although our skin was different, we were basically the same inside."

"You know Mimi, sometimes I think kids are smarter about things than grown-ups."

"I can't argue with you on that."

"I've been learning so much during

my trips back in time. I've met all of the Rosemarys."

"Except one," her grandmother reminded her.

"Mom! I forgot. But she didn't save postcards."

"No, she didn't, but I saved a postcard that she sent to me."

"Really? Where was it from? Can I go there?"

"Yes, you can go there. In fact, I think that you have to go there."

"I do? Why?"

"I'll tell you more later. The postcard is from Madrid, Spain. Your grandfather took your mother there during Thanksgiving break in 1975. Your mom was of course . . ."

"Ten!" interrupted Rosemary Rita.

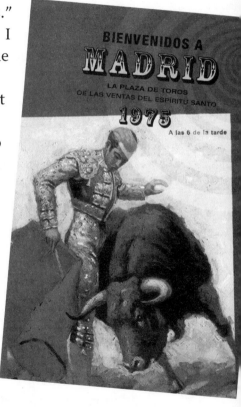

"You guessed it. Well, I'd better get going. I have a meeting in Sausalito in an hour. I'll call you tomorrow and we'll make plans."

"All right. 'Bye, Mimi. Love you."

"I love you too, dear."

Rosemary Rita hung up the phone and made a beeline to her room. She went straight to the pile of postcards and started going through them.

In a few minutes, she found it. The postcard from Madrid, Spain! Stapled to the card was a newspaper article from the *New York Times*. Sitting down on her bed to read the article, she thought, "I can't wait for tomorrow and my next adventure."

About the Author

*I have wished many times over the years that my
children could have known my grandmother, Mimi.
I am thrilled that her spirit comes to life in these books.
Now I can share Mimi with my own children and
many other children as well.*

—BARBARA ROBERTSON

Barbara Robertson lives in Greenville, South Carolina, with her husband, Marsh, and their three children, Ashley, Will, and Eileen. She has earned B.A. and M.A. degrees in Elementary and Early Childhood Education. A former teacher, Barbara enjoys volunteering at her children's schools. In addition, she serves on several community boards (Children's Hospital, Friends of the Greenville Zoo, and the South Carolina Children's Theatre). When she's not pounding on her word processor or chauffeuring her children, you might find Barbara on the tennis court or curled up with a good book.

Moraine Cay

Allans—Pensacola Cay

Spanish Cay

Powell Cay

Manjack Cay

Green Turtle Cay
(New Plymouth)

No Name Cay

Whale Cay

Great Guana Cay

Man 'O War Cay

Elbow Cay

Tilloo and Pelican Cays

Lynyard Cay

Little Harbour

N

12 miles

The Albacos

A GROUP OF ISLANDS
IN THE BAHAMAS

Mores Island

Hole in The Wall

A Note from the Author

Rosemary Rita picked the Green Turtle Cay postcard out of the stack because of the beautiful picture of turquoise blue water and white sandy beaches. Of course, once she read about the prospect of buried treasure it was too thrilling for her to pass up!

Green Turtle Cay is a real place. In fact, the tiny three-mile-long island is one of more than seven hundred islands that make up the Bahamas. It was given its name because of the many turtles that once lived on the island's beaches. (*Cay* is pronounced "key," and it means "low island, or reef of sand or coral.") Now, the namesake turtles are quite scarce, and are on the protected species list.

The village of New Plymouth, where Mimi and Viola were living, is located on the southern tip of the cay. It is home to just over five hundred persons. (Many of the current residents can trace their roots to Revolutionary War Loyalists—American colonists who migrated to the island because they were on the side of the British during the struggle for independence.) At the time of Rosemary Rita's visit, even fewer people lived there. There were no cars on the island. On land, people walked from place to place, and on water, they used dinghies or other small boats to travel from one island to the other. The New Plymouth Inn mentioned in this story really does exist today, though at the time this story would have taken place— 1947—it was still the private home of the Chamberlain family. As mentioned in the story, Neville Chamberlain was the British prime minister from 1937 through 1940, and for a time, he did live on Green Turtle Cay. His home there was renovated in 1954 and it became the first inn on the island.

This *Hourglass Adventure* takes place just after the end of World War II. During that war, nearly all Americans were involved in helping the war effort in some way. While the soldiers were off fighting, others went to work in factories making ammunition and other items needed by the troops. People made many sacrifices in order to support the war effort. But at this time, the Bahamas were still a British colony, and Green Turtle Cay was quite remote. Few people left or visited the area, though during the war, some of the island's young people served in the British armed forces.

After the war, people were happy to return to their regular lives. British and American spirits were high after the victorious outcome for the Allies. After years of sacrifice, people could begin to think about traveling by airplane or ship for pleasure once more. They wanted to enjoy life after the hard war years. Naturally, places such as Green Turtle Cay and the other Bahamian islands became alluring destinations for American tourists. Developers—people who take unspoiled land and build homes, apartments, office buildings, or, in the case of this story, hotels and casinos—could see the future opportunities in such a beautiful setting. Over the coming years, the Bahamas would grow to be a very attractive spot for vacationers.

Now, the islands are famous for their tropical weather, and visitors from all over the world flock to their beautiful beaches. While there, you can visit Mimi's house on Green Turtle Cay—a white clapboard with a red roof and green shutters. This house really does exist, and is actually the Albert Lowe Museum—one of the many wonderful places to visit on the island. The museum has fascinating photographs dating back to the turn of the century. It also has artifacts from life on the island, as well as the incredible ship models of Abaco sailing vessels that Viola mentions to Rosemary Rita. These ship models were built by Albert Lowe, a Green Turtle Cay ship builder—the man for whom the museum is named.

There is much to do on the Bahamian islands. In addition to the museum, you can also try water sports such as wind surfing, parasailing, jet skiing, and water skiing. Swimming, fishing, snorkeling, surfing, and scuba diving are also popular pastimes. Beneath the ocean surface, there is a whole world of aquatic life to explore. Tropical fish, eels, and coral reefs all make their home in the Bahamas's crystal clear waters.

Conch (pronounced "konk") is another animal that is plentiful in the ocean around the islands. Conch are a kind of mollusk—from the same family as snails—that are eaten in many different Bahamian recipes. Mrs. Cornish's famous conch fritters are just one way to prepare them. Conch can also be added to soups, stews, and salads, or eaten fried, raw, or steamed.

PIRATE LEGENDS AND TREASURE MAPS

The Bahamas are also famous for having been a port for pirates in the late 1600s to early 1700s. Nearby trade routes between the colonies and their parent countries in Europe were attractive bait for pirates. They would seize a ship loaded with goods or money in order to make their living. Many pirates bragged that they had buried treasures on the islands and rumors of these buried riches still persist to this day. The pirates found that the islands were a good hideout for themselves and their treasures. With over 700 islands to choose from, it was easy to find a hideaway.

One of the most famous pirates who sailed during this time was Blackbeard. Although Blackbeard was known for his ferocious ways, legend says that if his victims gave up their valuables without a fight, he would let them go without harm. However, if they fought back, he would leave the crew stranded by burning their ship—or worse!

Although many are aware of the famous male pirates, few know about the women who also terrorized the seas. Two in particular—Anne Bonny and Mary Read—were notorious for their fierce ways. Disguised as men, the women worked with the pirate Calico Jack, seizing the goods off of small merchant ships.

In addition to looking for treasure buried *on* the islands, people also search for valuables in the ocean that surrounds them. Off the coast of nearby Treasure Cay, a fleet of fifteen Spanish galleons filled with treasure crashed in the 1500s. Some of the goods remain hidden beneath the waters, and people are still hunting for them today.

BAHAMIAN CULTURE

From the mid-1600s to 1973, the Bahamas were a British colony—but a blend of many cultural traditions gives the Bahamas a personality all its own. In addition to the British influence, several other cultures have made an impact on the Bahamas. For instance, about 85 per cent of the population is of

African descent, and some of the traditions practiced by native Bahamians today have their roots in African cultures. Before British occupation, the country was also settled by the Spanish and French, who left their impact on the Bahamas.

Before the Europeans arrived, the land was inhabited by native people called the Lucayans, also known as the Arawak Indians. As Columbus and his explorers settled the Bahamian islands, the Lucayan people were pushed off their land and enslaved. Ultimately, they perished from the harsh treatment, but artifacts from their culture are still being found in archeological digs on the islands.

As Viola discovers in this *Hourglass* episode, slavery existed on the islands until 1834, when the practice was finally outlawed in the territory. The legacy of slavery still remains part of the culture of the islands. One of the country's most colorful holidays— Junkanoo—was originated by enslaved people who were given a few days off from work to celebrate the Christmas season with their families. It is believed that Junkanoo has its roots in African culture, and some think that the festival was named after an enslaved African man named "John Canoe" who refused to work on the Christmas holidays. These holidays grew into elaborate parties with music, costumes, and dance. The costumes are brightly colored, and feature enormous, detailed headdresses. Historically, the costumes were made from materials found in nature on the islands such as sea sponges and leaves. Now, they are made with materials such as crêpe paper, fabric, and cardboard.

If you're lucky enough to visit Green Turtle Cay on New Year's Day, you'll catch the Junkanoo Parade in all its splendor—but a visit to the Bahamas is a treat any time of year. While you're there, stop by the Albert Lowe Museum to learn more about Green Turtle Cay's fascinating history—and don't forget to taste those famous conch fritters!

Generation

Rosemary Ruth "Rosemarie" Berger (Christianson)
Great-great-great-grandmother

Rosemary Grace "Gracie" Christianson (Gibson)
Great-great-grandmother

Rosemary Anna "May May" Gibson (Ryan)
Great-grandmother

Rosemary Regina "Mimi" Ryan (Carlisle)
Grandmother

Rosemary Leigh Carlisle (Hampton)
Mother

Rosemary Rita Hampton

# of Rosemarys

BORN	AGE 10
1860	1870
1879	1889
1909	1919
1937	1947
1965	1975
1991	2001

WHAT'S NEXT?

Read a chapter from Rosemary Rita's next adventure at winslowpress.com